CALEB'S KITTENS

Written by Katie Nagy

Illustrated by Isla Celestine Studio

A Note to Parents:

Katie began fostering animals when a mother cat and her four newborn kittens showed up on her patio in 2007. Since then, she and her family have fostered not only kittens, but also adult cats and dogs and senior animals through various animal welfare organizations.

While Caleb and Emily love helping foster kittens, it can prove to be a tough and emotional job. Sometimes kittens are sick or have unknown issues and don't always survive. Despite this, it is so rewarding to see them grow up and move on to new families. There are many ways you can help animals in need. Caleb's special superpower in the story stems from his neurodiversity and he proves that every person can use their own personal talents and skills to make a difference in the world. At the back of this book, you can find some of the resources that can help you find your local animal welfare organization and start learning about how you can use your family's special skills to help animals in need.

Copyright

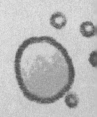

Dedication

This book is dedicated to Caleb, Emily and all the amazing kids who are committed to caring for animals, and each other, with kindness.

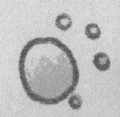

Proverbs 12:10a

"The righteous care for the needs of their animals"

This is the very true story of a little boy named Caleb and his search for a little lost kitten.

Caleb has had tiny kittens in his home for as long as he can remember.

Many kittens are brought into the shelter who have been born outside and accidentally separated from their mother cat.

Other kittens are brought to the shelter who have been born to someone's pet cat and they don't have the space to keep them all.

The kittens need to go live in foster homes for several weeks because they are too young to be placed into new families.

The foster families make sure the kittens grow up healthy and strong and teach them how to be good pets.

Before the kittens can be adopted into a forever family, they must be big enough to have a special surgery that will make sure they can't have kittens of their own.

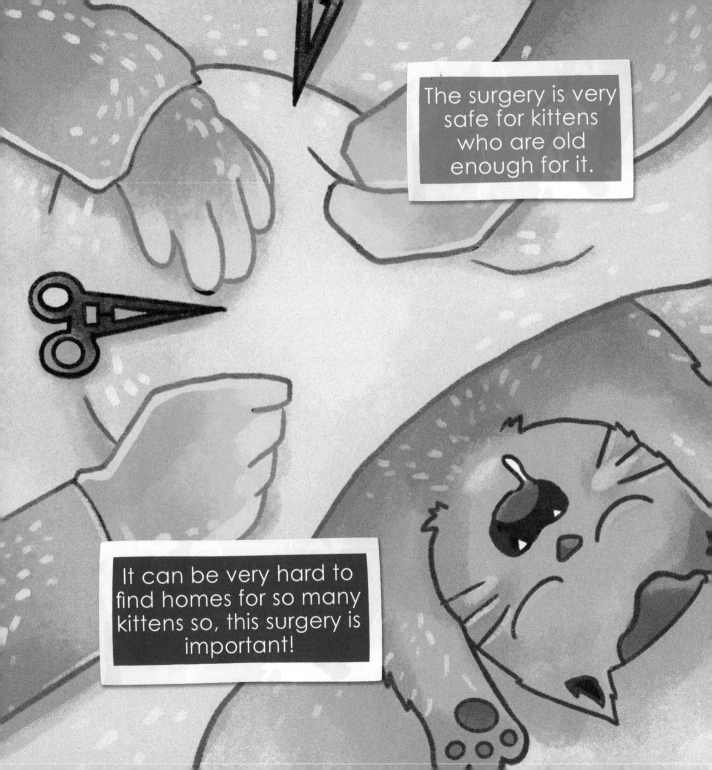

He helps feed them and clean their kitten cage. He and his little sister, Emily, also play with them and help to make sure they are used to being around people.

After a few weeks at his house, Caleb's mom takes the kittens back to the shelter where the veterinarian performs the special surgery and then the kittens get to go home with new forever families.

Caleb's mom brings home a new litter of kittens right away, so they have a whole new batch of little furry friends to care for.

One of Caleb's favorite things about the kittens is how soft they are. Caleb is a super awesome kind of kid who loves all soft things!

Caleb's mom says that the special way Caleb thinks and feels is his superpower!

Caleb's mom searched the basement, where there are a lot of hiding places a small kitten can fit into.

Even Emily helped by looking under the couch.

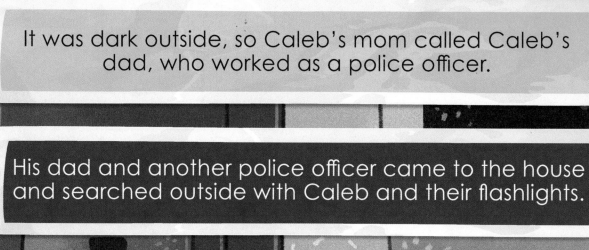

It was dark outside, so Caleb's mom called Caleb's dad, who worked as a police officer.

His dad and another police officer came to the house and searched outside with Caleb and their flashlights.

The search went on until every possible spot in the house and yard were checked. Or, so they thought...

Just as Caleb's mom was about to call the shelter to tell them Scottie was lost, something amazing happened!

She saw Scottie's eyes flash in the reflection of the glass of the t.v. cabinet!

Scottie had been hiding there the whole time, watching everyone search for him in a panic!

Caleb, his mom, Emily, and the police officers were all so relieved to have found little Scottie.
They laughed at how silly the tiny kitten had been!

That day, Caleb learned how important it is to keep a very close watch on little kittens when they are so young and small.

Scottie grew up, got that special surgery from the veterinarian and found a forever home and family.

Caleb and his family still work together to take very good care of all the tiny, soft and quiet kittens.

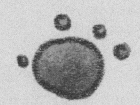
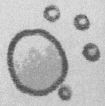

Kathryn (Katie) Nagy was born and raised in Philadelphia, PA. She received her Bachelors of Arts degree in Psychology in 2004 and her Masters of Arts degree in Counseling Psychology along with her PA School Counseling certification in 2006. Katie worked as a high school counselor in Philadelphia from 2006-2018 until she filled the role of Humane Educator at the Montgomery County SPCA. Here, Katie travels all over the county teaching both kids and adults about the various animal welfare issues facing our world today. She is especially passionate about the plight of pet overpopulation and the importance of living in harmony with neighborhood wildlife. Katie obtained her Certified Humane Education Specialist credential in 2020 through The Academy of ProSocial Learning and is a member of the Association of Professional Humane Educators.

Katie currently lives in Abington, PA with her husband, Bill, and their children, Caleb and Emily. Their family shares their home with their two dogs, two cats and two box turtles and of course, all the furry little foster friends that come in and out of their lives!

Katie Nagy
The Author

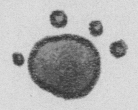

Resources

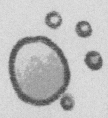

Pet Overpopulation occurs when there are more pets available than there are suitable and willing homes to care for them. This results in the euthanasia of healthy, adoptable pets. According to the ASPCA, 6.5 million companion animals enter US shelters every year and 1.5 million of them are euthanized. For more details on Pet-Overpopulation, please visit:
https://www.aspca.org/animal-homelessness/shelter-intake-and-surrender/pet-statistics

Spaying and neutering your pets is the best way to prevent pet-overpopulation. If you are local to the Philadelphia area and would like to find resources on this or any other type of help with your pet, please contact:
https://www.phillynokill.org/

If you want to find an animal shelter or rescue across the US in order to volunteer, foster or adopt an animal, visit:
https://www.petfinder.com/animal-shelters-and-rescues/

Would you like to learn more about how to foster kittens? Check out the link below.
https://kittencoalition.org/

Made in the USA
Middletown, DE
26 November 2021

53062058R00024